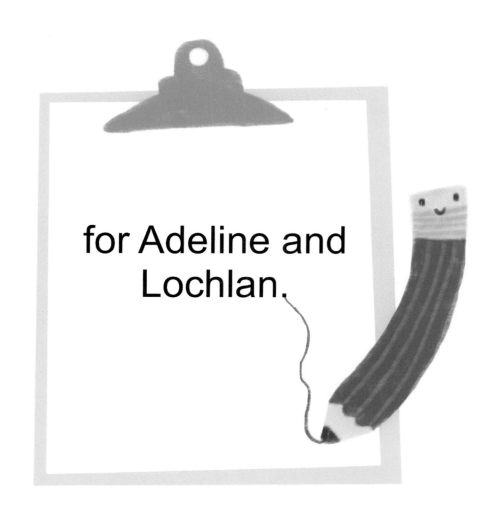

for Adeline and Lochlan.

This book belongs to

If your leg breaks
or hip groans, my
mum will help,

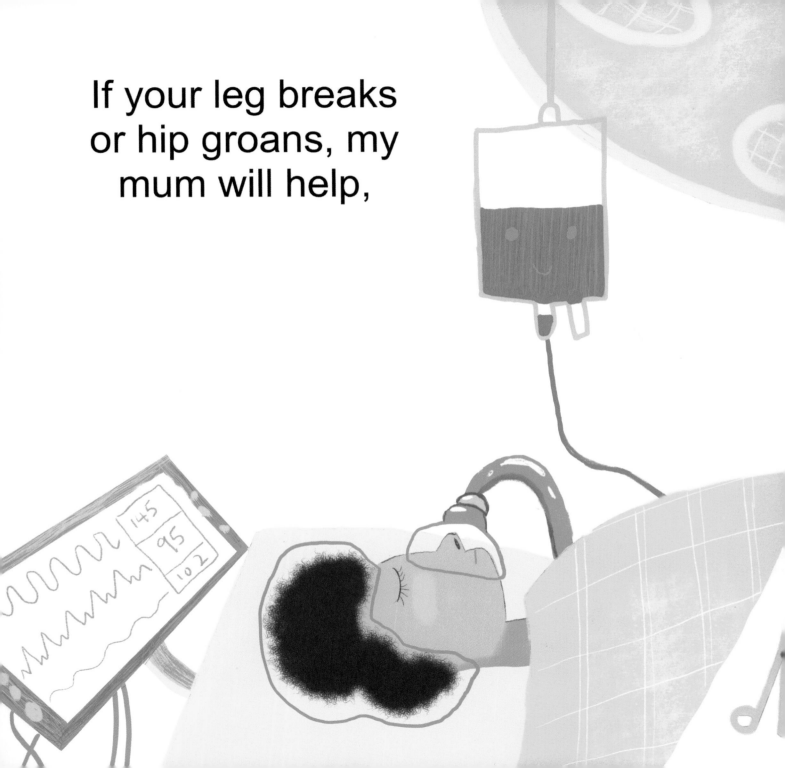

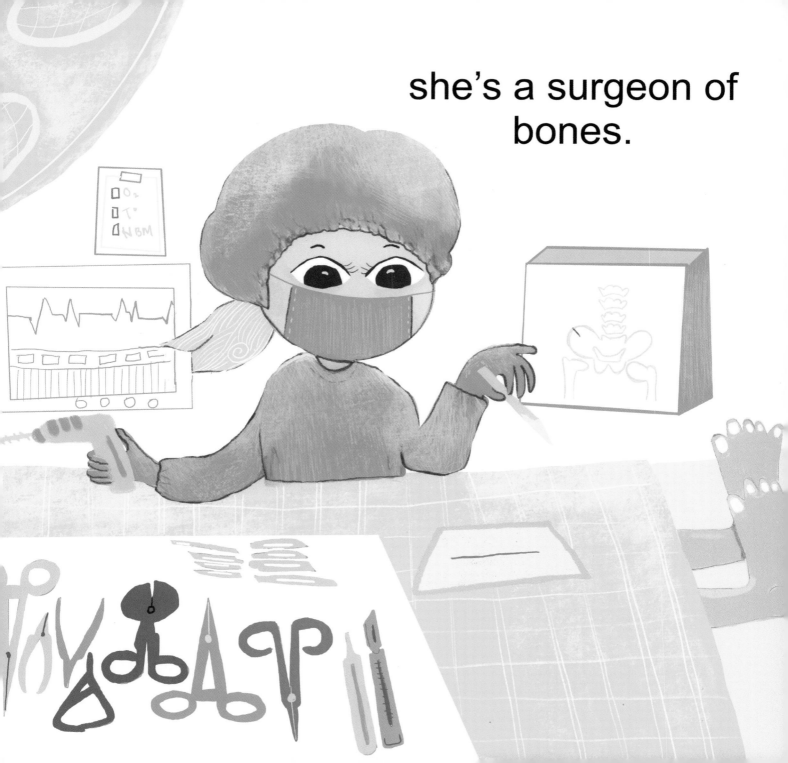

she's a surgeon of bones.

What does your mum do?

My mum's trying
to work out if
aliens exist,

she's an
astrophysicist.

What does your mum do?

My mum builds skyscrapers high into the atmosphere,

she's a civil engineer.

My mum makes important decisions and is always on the go,

Dad says she's "the big boss",

she's a CEO.

What does your mum do?

My mum looks at potions, magic and mists,

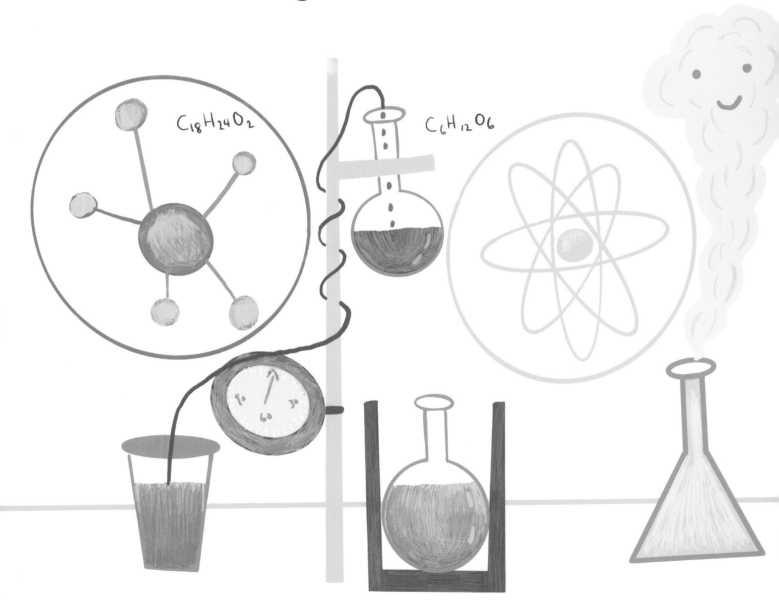

She works in a lab
as a scientist.

What does your
mum do?

My mum makes dragons fly and fills their mouths with flames.

She's a software developer, making awesome video games.

What does YOUR mum do?

My mum is in charge of all these sheep, making sure they get home safely to sleep.

What will you do?

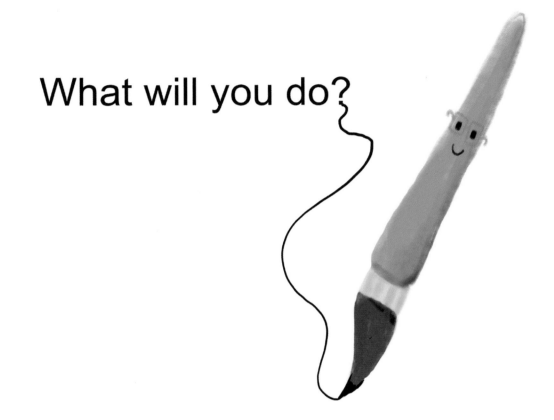

Printed in Poland
by Amazon Fulfillment
Poland Sp. z o.o., Wrocław

58671507R00021